I LOVE YOU PAST IMAGINE

BRI AMARO

To order additional copies of this book, contact:
Xlibris
844-714-8691
www.Xlibris.com
Orders@Xlibris.com

ISBN: Softcover   978-1-6641-9121-1
         Hardcover   978-1-6641-9122-8
         EBook   978-1-6641-9120-4

Print information available on the last page

Rev. date: 08/26/2021

ABOUT THE BOOK:

This book was inspired by my oldest son, Nicholas. We read books every night when he was little, and after we would always play the "I love you game". One night he tried to outsmart me and said he loved me past imagine. When I asked what that meant, he said, "I love you past what you could ever imagine". This then became the way we always said goodnight. He is now close to adulthood and every night before I head to bed, I peek my head into his room and say, "I love you past imagine, and I always will". - Mom

This book belongs to:

_____

Mom- "Goodnight sweetheart it's time to sleep".

Mom- "I love you more than the toes on your feet".

Son- "I love you more than the bubbles in my bath".

Mom- "I love you more than big belly laughs".

Son- "I love you more than the planes flying high".

Mom- "I love you more than all the stars in the sky".

Son- "I love you more than all the trees on our street".

Mom- "I love you more than all the fish swimming deep".

Son- "I love you more than all the noodles in my soup".

Mom- "I love you more than a thousand hula hoops".

Son- "I love you more than warm apple pie".

Mom- "I love you more than the mountains high".

Son- "I love you more than winning first place".

Mom- "I love you more than all the freckles on your face".

Son- "I love you more than my big comfy bed".

Mom- "I love you more than all the hairs on your head".

Son- "I love you more than the softest teddy bear".

Mom- "I'll tuck you to bed with extra special care".

Mom- "I love you past imagine and you know that's why,
I'll love you forever my perfect little guy".

The End